P9-DDL-958

MEOW RUFF

WRITTEN BY JOYCE SIDMAN
ILLUSTRATED BY MICHELLE BERG

Houghton Mifflin Company
Boston 2006

www.houghtonmifflinbooks.com

Book design by Michelle Berg.
The text of this book is set in: ATQuay Sans, Cafeteria,
Frankfurt Ultra Laser, Impact, Sassoon Primary, & Typewriter.
The illustrations were created in Adobe Photoshop & Adobe Illustrator.

Library of Congress Cataloging-in-Publication Data

Sidman, Joyce.
Meow Ruff / by Joyce Sidman; illustrations by Michelle Berg.
p. cm.
ISBN 0-618-44894-2 (hardcover)
1. Children's poetry, American. I. Berg, Michelle. II. Title.
PS3569.I295M46 2005
811'.54-dc22
2004027206

ISBN-13: 978-0618-44894-4

Manufactured in CHINA
SCP 10 9 8 7 6 5 4 3 2 1

To
Ann Rider,
for her vision, heart,
and endless patience.
J.S.
With love to my parents,
Dr. Charles & Joy Berg,
who are always there for me.
Ric, thanks for the guidance.
And to Judy Sue,
my teacher & friend.
M.B.

WITHDRAWN

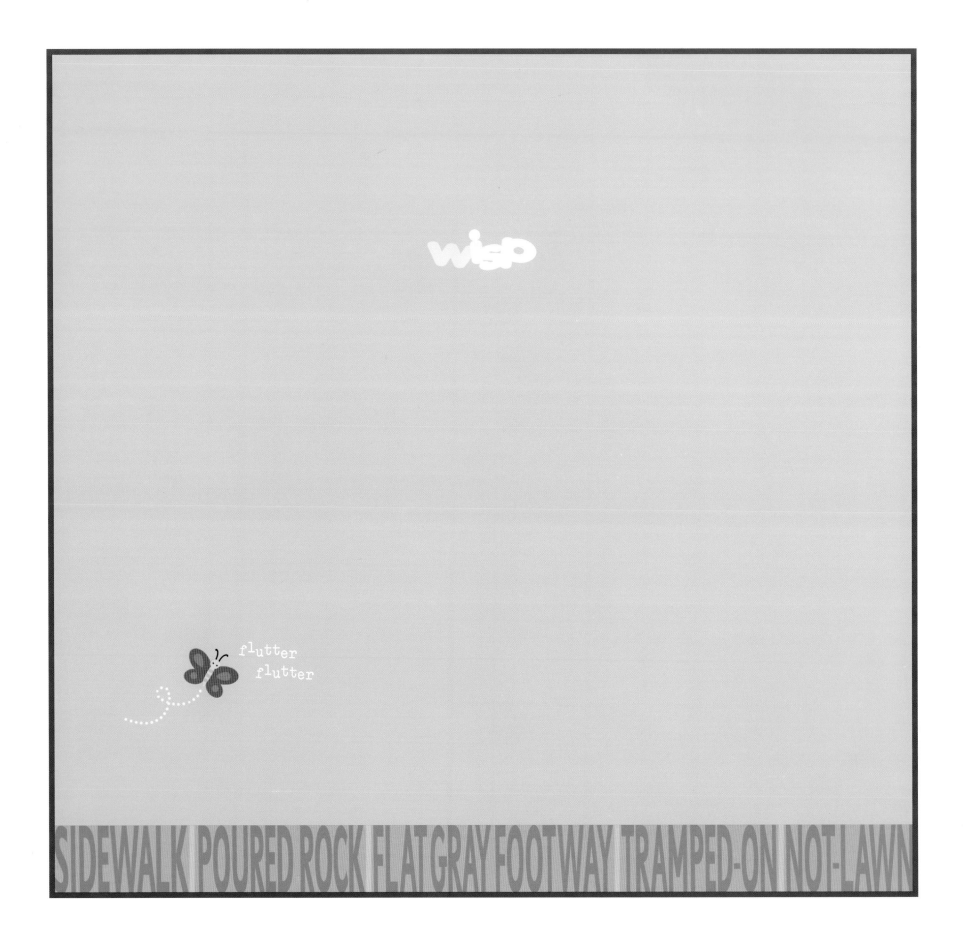

wisp

flutter
flutter

SIDEWALK POURED ROCK FLAT GRAY FOOTWAY TRAMPED-ON NOT-LAWN

caw

CROWS RULE

lowly cat

EACH
LEAF
A MAP OF
BRANCHES
EACH TWIG
A BRANCH
OF LEAVES
EACH BRANCH
A TREE OF TWIGS
EACH TREE
A GREEN
HAIRED
SLIM
CHESTED
GREAT
HEARTED GNARL-ARMED
STRONG
LEGGED
DEEP-ROOTED
ONE

delicate footsteps—must not get feet wet

PETUNIA-EDGED, MUCH-FLATTENED, STURDY-BLADED, SEED-STUDDED GRASS

CHURNING CLUMPS OF LUSTROUS
GLOSS-TOPPED CREAM
CHARGING ROLLING ROLLICKING
GATHERING GROWING GALLOPING
BUNCHED AND BLUSTEROUS
THICK AND THICKER
WHIPPED AND WHIRLING
HEAVY AND HEAVIE

dog vs. cat

sniff snuffle SNEEZE! is that . . . ?

At last At last—
CAT!

and not all ladies

but really beetles

safe at last!

lady bugs

SWEET.TICKLISH.SAP-MOSS.____.FEATHERY.EARTH-SMELL.MEADOW-PINE.SUN

THUNDER-PLUMPED SEETHIN

BLACK-BOTTOMEI

d
r
i
p

EACH LEAF
DIPPING AND DANCING
EACH TWIG
THRASHING
AND PLUNGIN
EACH BRANC
BENDING TO SHOW
SILVERY
UNDERSIDE
AND D
THE

Scary Hissing Cat!

SLIM
CHESTED
GREAT
HEARTED
STRONG GNARL-ARMED
LEGGED
DEEP-ROOTED
ONE
SWAYS
SLIGHTLY

follow me

flee for cover

rain coming

DEEPENING, DARKENING, SHADOW-LADEN, MYSTERIOUS, JUNGLE-GLADE GREEN

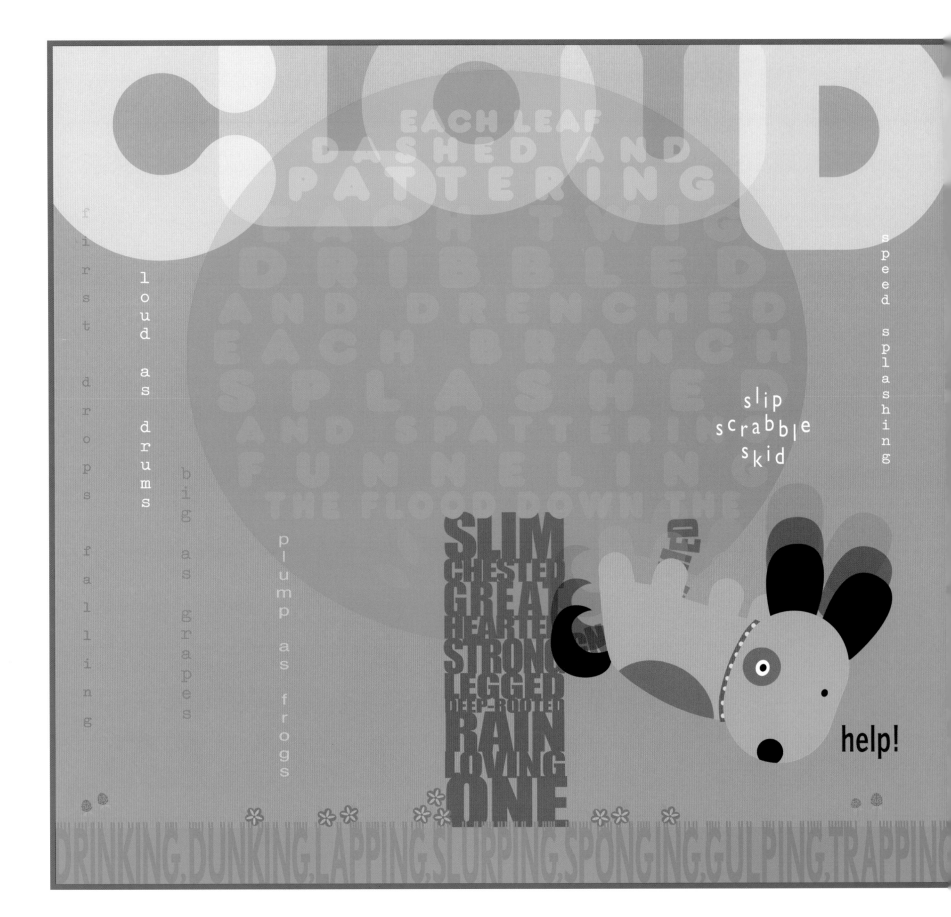

CLOUD

EACH LEAF
DASHED AND
PATTERING

EACH TWIG
DRIBBLED
AND DRENCHED
EACH BRANCH
SPLASHED
AND SPATTERING
FUNNELING
THE FLOOD DOWN THE

first drops falling

loud as drums

big as grapes

plump as frogs

speed splashing

slip
scrabble
skid

SLIM
CHESTED
GREAT
HEARTED
STRONG
LEGGED
DEEP-ROOTED
RAIN
LOVING
ONE

help!

DRINKING. DUNKING. LAPPING. SLURPING. SPONGING. GULPING. TRAPPING

LOOSE BUNDLES
SHIFTING TUMBLING
PARTING

fat fingers tip tapping

PLATFORM THAT'S SPLOTTING AND SPLATTING AND DRIPPING

snore snuggle   purrrr snuggle

HAIL-FROSTED, CRYSTAL-TWINKLING, FAST-MELTING, SOPPING SOUP OF SLUSH

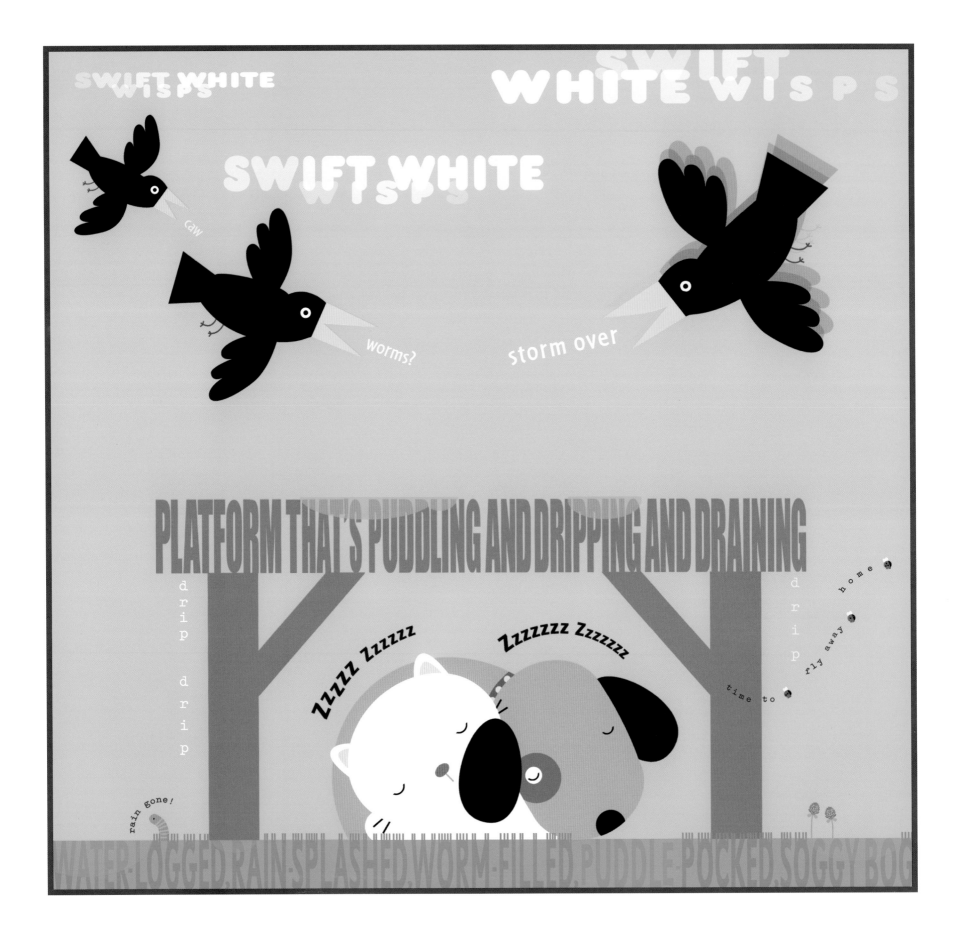

"There
you are,
pup...

Have you
found
a friend ?"